A DAY IN AN ECOSYSTEM

24 HOURS IN THE OCEAN

LAURA L. SULLIVAN

Cavendish Square
New York

Published in 2018 by Cavendish Square Publishing, LLC
243 5th Avenue, Suite 136, New York, NY 10016

CPSIA Compliance Information: Batch #CS17CSQ

All websites were available and accurate when this book was sent to press.

Library of Congress Cataloging-in-Publication Data

Names: Sullivan, Laura L., 1974- author.
Title: 24 hours in the ocean / Laura L. Sullivan.
Other titles: Twenty-four hours in the ocean
Description: New York : Cavendish Square Publishing, 2018. | Series: A day in an ecosystem | Includes index.
Identifiers: LCCN 2016049572 (print) | LCCN 2016055749 (ebook) | ISBN 9781502624789 (library bound) | ISBN 9781502624772 (E-book)
Subjects: LCSH: Marine ecology--Juvenile literature. | Ocean--Juvenile literature.
Classification: LCC QH541.5.S3 S96 2018 (print) | LCC QH541.5.S3 (ebook) |DDC 577.7--dc23
LC record available at https://lccn.loc.gov/2016049572

Editorial Director: David McNamara
Editor: Fletcher Doyle
Copy Editor: Rebecca Rohan
Associate Art Director: Amy Greenan
Designer: Stephanie Flecha
Production Coordinator: Karol Szymczuk
Photo Research: J8 Media

Printed in the United States of America

CONTENTS

DAWN

AS you float on a calm **ocean**, the star-filled sky begins to grow lighter. To the east, a pale pink blush appears on the **horizon**. In a few moments, the sun will rise. For now, the ocean creatures are in the in-between time at the edge of night and day. Animals that are active at **twilight**, around dawn and dusk, are called **crepuscular**.

On the land, choruses of birds are greeting the coming day with songs. Scientists have recently discovered that below the waves, some species "sing" every dawn, too. The ocean is not a silent place. Many fish, shrimp, and marine **mammals** make noises to communicate, to mark their **territory**, and to find mates. Fish make grunts, squeaks, gurgles, and pops. The sounds can be especially loud just before the sun comes up.

Every night, there is a huge **migration** from the ocean depths toward the surfaces. (You will learn more about this in the Evening chapter.) As the sun begins to come up, the **zooplankton** that rose to feed in the warmer

As the sun rises, some animals, such as these dolphins, jump into action.

Grunts and other fish "sing" during the dawn hours.

waters near the surface start to sink down again. They take with them all of the **nutrients** they gathered in the rich waters nearer the sunlight.

Dawn is a time for the changing of the guard, when **nocturnal** animals are getting ready to rest, and **diurnal** animals are about to start their activities. Therefore, it is a perfect time for **predators** to be on the move.

At dawn, they have access to both nighttime and daytime **prey**.

Some people believe that most shark attacks happen at dawn and dusk. A recent study in Australia disproved this belief. Sharks do actively hunt at dawn, but most sharks will hunt at any time of the day or night. The majority of shark bites happen during the day when people are most likely to be swimming. You are more likely to get bitten when visibility is low, such as in cloudy water or at night.

At dawn, when the sun rises, the water slowly begins to heat. As a **warm-blooded** human, your body makes its own heat, keeping you at a constant temperature. Most fish are **cold-blooded**. The water temperature sets their body temperature. Muscles work better when they are warmer. So a fish that needs speed and agility to hunt is often more effective in warmer water.

In shallower water near the shore, the temperature difference between night and day is more dramatic. If you see a snook—a popular

GOOD MORNING DOLPHINS!

Dolphins never get a good night's sleep. That's because dolphins can only let half of their brain go to sleep at a time. All dolphins and whales need to be conscious to breathe. So when they sleep, they have to keep half of their brain awake enough to decide when they should breathe. If they didn't, they might slip under the water and drown.

Some shallow-water fish like the snook wait for the sun to warm the water so they can be faster and more active when they hunt.

sport and food fish—before dawn, it will be sluggish. However, once the sun comes up and warms the water and the snook's muscles, the fish will be lively and fast.

If you are on the deep, open ocean at dawn, you will see many **pelagic** fish that have scattered at night come together in **schools**. In the dark, fish like herring and sardines are safer from predators. As the sunlight shines through the water, though, you can clearly see their silver forms. So can predators. In the daylight, pelagic fish form huge schools to help keep them safe from predators. Many schooling fish such as cod have their main feeding period at dawn.

MORNING

IMAGINE you are taking a voyage out to sea. It is early morning, with a clear sky and a gentle breeze that is slowly getting stronger. By the afternoon, the heat coming off the land will meet moist ocean air and create thunderstorms, but for now, the weather is perfect for observing marine life.

Where the ocean waves hit the shore in the **intertidal** zone, between high and low tide, the bivalves such as clams that were safe overnight suddenly have to dig down to avoid the shorebirds that now hunt them. A little deeper, sheepshead are starting to forage around the rocks and piers for their favorite food, barnacles.

As you travel out to sea, you see other mammals leaving the safety of shore to brave the ocean in search of food. If you were off the coast of South Africa near Seal Island in November or December, you would see large numbers of brown fur seals gathered on the rocky shore. Males have established territories on the beaches, and females are giving birth

Shorebirds hunt for tiny clams and crustaceans in the intertidal zone in the morning.

Seals gather by the thousands on Seal Island to have their pups.

to their pups. Early in the morning, you will see groups of mother seals go out to sea to hunt for fish and squid. They will be gone for several days. However, between the safe shore and the open ocean, danger and death awaits.

Great white sharks are huge, reaching up to 20 feet (6.1 meters) and 4,300 pounds (1,950 kilograms). During seal breeding season they cruise around Seal Island in what is known as the "ring of death." All seals leaving the island have to pass by hungry sharks.

Great white sharks lunge from the deep and even leap from the water as they hunt seals.

Under the bright light of morning, you see a dozen seals lumber off the rocks and plunge into the water. On shore, their pups will wait for several days until their mothers return to nurse them if they ever return. Seals use different survival strategies. Some of the seals plunge down to hide near the murky bottom. They are harder to see but have less room to move to escape. You see other seals swim swiftly near the surface. They shoot like arrows, breaching for a quick breath.

Then, suddenly, you see a huge fin cutting through the water. A great white shark has spotted one of the seals. The seal begins to zigzag frantically

Dolphin fish have the same name as the mammal that is also called a dolphin.

DOLPHIN FISH AND DOLPHIN MAMMALS

The fish with the scientific name *Coryphaena hippurus* has a misleading common name. Many people refer to it as a dolphin. (Other names are dorado or mahi-mahi.) It is not at all related to the marine mammal also called a dolphin. The mahi-mahi is a fish. It might have been named for the way its bulbous head surges through the waves when it hunts, making it look a little like a dolphin.

as the shark pursues her. The shark is bigger, and probably faster, but the little seal is more **agile**. When the shark gets close, she darts behind the shark and hides behind the shark's **dorsal** fin. No matter how the shark twists and turns, it can't reach the seal. Eventually it gives up, and you think the seal is safe.

Neither you nor the seal see the second great white shark until it is too late. This one uses the shark's favorite hunting strategy. From deep below it rockets straight up at 25 miles per hour (40 kilometers per hour) and smashes into the seal with its toothy jaws wide open. The lunge is so powerful that you see the shark shoot 10 feet (3 m) out of the water. The great white then quickly eats its prey before other hungry sharks intrude.

As the morning progresses, you leave Seal Island behind and go farther out to sea. As you go out, heading against a stiffening breeze, you see other sailors on the surface of the water, coming toward you. They have beautiful air-

The Portuguese man-o-war depends on the wind to sail on the ocean's surface.

filled floats in vibrant shades of blue and purple. The top of the float is shaped like a sail that seems to catch the wind as if on a miniature sailboat. Below the water, you can see their **tentacles** drifting as much as 98 feet (30 m). They are Portuguese man-o-war. Though they look like jellyfish, they are actually siphonophores. Instead of being one animal, they are a colony of individualized animals that can only survive when they are joined together.

Each part, or polyp, does a job. Some are for feeding, others for reproduction. The tentacle polyps are covered in stinging **nematocysts**. Just below the waves, you can see a silver fish covered in black blotches swimming near the tentacles. You think the fish is doomed. But it seems

Flying fish leap from the water and glide to escape predators such as mahi-mahi.

FLYING FISH

The flying fish lives in the open ocean, and has many predators. To help them escape, they have **evolved** fins that resemble wings. They can't actually fly, but they can leap out of the water and glide for long distances—as many as 1,300 feet (400 m). They can glide up to 43 miles per hour (70 kph) and stay in the air a maximum of 45 seconds.

unharmed and even takes a nibble at the man-o-war. It is a man-o-war fish. It is immune to stings from the least **toxic** tentacles and agile enough to avoid the dangerous ones.

Suddenly, you see a small school of squid. They change color as they swim. At first, you think it is just the sunlight dancing on their skin. Soon, you realize that these squid can change their colors and patterns at will. So can most other squid and octopus. They can use the colors as **camouflage**, warning, and possibly as a form of communication. Most of the squid dodge the tentacles, but one is snagged and is almost instantly paralyzed. The tentacle drags the squid up to the digestive polyps.

From close by, you hear a puff of breath. A 400-pound (181 kg) loggerhead sea turtle has come up for air. It is hunting the man-o-war. The loggerhead is one of the few animals that can make a meal of a man-o-war. The skin on its mouth and throat are so thick that the nematocysts can't penetrate. Most sea turtles

Turtles have such thick skin that jellyfish stings don't bother them.

feast on jellyfish and siphonophores. Many sea turtles are sickened or killed each year from accidentally eating clear plastic garbage that looks like jellyfish.

AFTERNOON

IT is afternoon now as you continue to sail out into the ocean. Nearer to shore, thunderstorms are building as hot air from the land meets the incoming cooler, wet sea breeze. But out here, the sky is mostly a clear, vivid blue, with only a trace of the dappled clouds they call "mackerel sky" on the horizon. The clouds look like cotton balls in the air.

Speaking of mackerel, you see a school of Spanish mackerel swimming swiftly beneath your boat. Their speckled sides are an example of disruptive coloration. It breaks up their outline and makes them less visible to both their prey and any predators hunting them. Mackerel, and many other kinds of pelagic fish, also employ a coloring known as **countershading.** They are darker on the top of their bodies, and lighter colored or silvery on their bellies. An animal looking from beneath them will see them against the bright, sunlit surface, and their pale or shiny bodies will blend in with the light. But when you look down on them from above, their darker backs are

Many pelagic fish, sharks, and even dolphins use countershading to hide in the open water, with dark colors on top, light colors on the bottom.

Huge bluefin tuna keep parts of their bodies warmer than the water around them.

camouflaged against the dark ocean depths. Many other ocean animals have countershading, including bottlenose dolphins, herring, many species of sharks, and even black and white penguins.

The streamlined, fast-swimming mackerel look like they're headed somewhere specific, so you follow them. After a while, you see other fish in a similar shape, but much bigger. They are bluefin tuna. The largest can get up to 15 feet (4.5 m) long and weigh more than 1,000 pounds (454 kg). They are strong, very fast, predatory fish. Body heat is what helps them be so powerful. While most fish are cold-blooded and are the

The opah, or moonfish, is the first known warm-blooded fish.

same temperature as the water around them, tuna (and some mackerel sharks) can keep their core body temperature higher than that of the water. Their body is designed to conserve heat, so very little is lost to the environment. They can keep important parts like their muscles, eyes, and brain warm.

Up ahead, you can see that the surface of the water is churning and frothy. As you get closer, you see small silvery shapes leaping desperately out of the water. The mackerel and tuna are all headed directly for a big **bait ball**.

Just a short while ago, the baitfish were schooling loosely, far below the surface. Schools are a good defense against predators, because the fish can collectively watch for danger, and the large numbers make it less likely that any one fish will be eaten. But when schooling fish panic, their final

When schooling fish panic, they form a defensive bait ball.

A WARM-BLOODED FISH

Recently, scientists found the first truly warm-blooded fish. The moonfish, or opah, is a deepwater fish that is disk-shaped and can reach 100 pounds (45 kg). Its large pectoral [side] fins move quickly, generating heat that its efficient body conserves. Even in the cold water 1,000 feet (305 m) below the surface, the opah has a body temperature about 9 degrees Fahrenheit (5 degrees Celsius) higher than the surrounding water. This helps it move quickly to catch fish and squid.

defense is to form a bait ball. These fish were actually herded by a **pod** of dolphins. The dolphins chased them up toward the surface, using splashes and bubbles to scare them in the right direction. Crowded up against the "wall" of air, the baitfish had no choice but to make a bait ball.

Swordfish charge into bait balls and use their bills to slash fish.

Now, you can see the predators cooperating. They all have a common goal—to eat as much as possible. So they work together to keep the bait ball tight. When the tuna arrive, the dolphins move away to let them muscle through the center of the bait ball. The dolphins then eat the fish that get separated from the main mass. Swordfish arrive, slashing at the baitfish with their bills.

While the school was orderly, the bait ball is chaos. The small fish flee from the surface, and do their best to get to the middle of the ball. You see the ball churning as the fish strive for the best position. Every time a predator breaks up the bait ball it forms again, although smaller than before.

Suddenly, you see the dolphins and tuna scatter. Nearby, bubbles make the surface look like a pot of boiling water. You see more bubbles and soon see a pattern. The bubbles are forming a ring around the baitfish, frightening them, forcing them into an even tighter ball. What could be big enough to make so many bubbles?

Thresher sharks use their long tails to whip and stun their prey

THRESHER SHARKS

The thresher is a pelagic shark with a tail fin that is almost as long as its body. When it hunts in a bait ball, it rushes in and swings its long tail like a whip. The force generated stuns the baitfish. Then the thresher turns around to eat the helpless fish.

Soon the answer becomes clear. With a mighty splash, a **behemoth** surges from the depths in the center of the bubble net, its mouth wide open. Two more rise next to the first, their throats swollen with hundreds of gallons of water and thousands of fish. They are humpback whales, working together to get the biggest meal possible. As they sink back

Humpback whales make bubble nets to herd bait fish into a tight ball, so they can swallow hundreds at a time..

under the surface you see them strain out the water though their comb-like **baleen**, keeping their bounty of baitfish. The baleen is a tough material that hangs from the upper jaw of whales, like the humpback, that don't have teeth.

A while later the sun is sinking slowly in the west, and the ocean is calm again. A few smaller mackerel remain to eat the remaining baitfish, but the big predators have left. You can see things sinking slowly toward the bottom—scales, scraps of flesh, wounded and dead bait fish, and the feces of the animals that were recently feeding. These bits of animal matter are called **detritus**. Over the course of several hours or days, the detritus will descend to the depths, bringing nutrients and energy to a place that never sees the sun. The animals in the deepest parts of the oceans depend on the sinking detritus for food. Sometimes, huge whale carcasses will descend to the bottom. Bacteria and fungi can break down organic matter into tiny, nutrient-rich matter. An event called an upwelling carries this matter from the bottom of the ocean to the surface, where it nourishes the **phytoplankton**.

The deepest parts of the ocean are miles deep. The deepest, the Mariana Trench in the Pacific Ocean, is 36,070 feet (10,994 m) deep. This is nearly 7 miles.

EVENING

THE sun is now sinking low on the horizon. The sky lights up in intense shades of red and pink and gold. You begin to feel a little sleepy, but all around you, you see signs that the ocean world is not ready for sleep.

The bait ball you witnessed earlier is gone, and you think the predators have no reason to linger in the area. However, you still see dolphins circling lazily as if they were waiting for something. Flashes of fins at the surface tell you that sharks are still around, too. One giant shape with a broad, toothless mouth can only be a whale shark, largest of the fish. Other fish move into the area, too. What could they all be waiting for?

Your boat has **sonar** on it, and you scan the ocean depths. Just a little while ago, your instruments showed that the ocean bottom was at about 10,000 feet (3,048 m) below you. To your surprise, the bottom now seems to be at only 5,000 feet (1,524 m) ...then 4,000 feet (1,219 m). Gradually, the

The sun is sinking, and some predators are ready for rest.

Zooplankton, and the creatures that eat them, travel to the surface every night, and sink back down during the day

bottom seems to be getting closer to the surface. You haven't changed locations, and the ocean bottom isn't actually rising. What is happening?

You are witnessing the planet's biggest migration. Far bigger than the wildebeest migration in Africa, or the monarch butterfly migration from the United States to Mexico, the nightly ocean migration from the depths to the surface involves billions upon billions of organisms. Creatures move

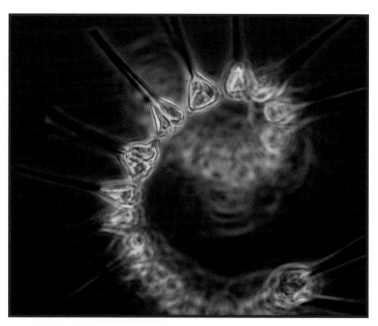

Phytoplankton live near the surface where they can use the sun for photosynthesis.

For creatures as tiny as zooplankton, swimming up though the water column every night is the equivalent of you walking 25 miles (40 km) or more for your breakfast. The effort required to swim through the water is about the same as if you tried to swim through thick molasses.

in such great numbers that they create a rising wall that can confuse the most advanced sonar. The wall of migrating animals is so great that submarines have even hidden beneath it, as safe from enemy sonar as if they were behind a steel wall.

Plankton are tiny, sometimes microscopic, creatures that live in the water column and cannot swim against currents. Algae, bacteria, protozoans, and even small invertebrates such as shrimp make up plankton. So do the eggs and larvae of crustaceans, worms, and even fish. Phytoplankton are plantlike plankton that use photosynthesis to get their energy from the sun. They have to live in the sunlit zone of the ocean. This layer extends down to a maximum of 656 feet (200 m). Most phytoplankton live even shallower, where they can get more sunlight, and thus more energy. Most of the ocean's creatures live in the sunlit zone. Phytoplankton are the primary producers in the ocean's food web.

Zooplankton (animal plankton) live throughout the oceans, but the majority spend their days in the depths. At night, though, they travel upward in a process called diel vertical migration. They make this nightly journey—diel means it involves a period of twenty-four hours—for several reasons. The ultraviolet light produced by the sun is a kind of radiation that can sometimes harm zooplankton. Ultraviolet light is what can give you a sunburn. Zooplankton are also at risk. By staying deep, far away from the sun during daylight hours, they avoid potentially harmful ultraviolet radiation.

Because most predators live near the surface, zooplankton are more vulnerable whenever they rise. Staying below for part of the day reduces their odds of being eaten. Also, they are much more visible in the bright light. Many of the things that eat zooplankton are visual hunters. They

Zooplankton rise at night to eat the phytoplankton that live near the surface.

need to see what they are going after. Hiding in the ocean depths during the day provides more protection from predators. But they still need to eat phytoplankton to survive. So when evening comes and the light fades, zooplankton start to rise through the water column. At night, they can feast on phytoplankton while being in less danger themselves. On dark nights, they go very near the surface. During the full moon, however, they rise but stay lower down, away from the glare.

You can see the ocean around you growing cloudy from the many zooplankton that now swarm the water near the surface. Some fish and other organisms from the depths have followed the zooplankton upward. As you look at the assortment of creatures around you, you can see an entire food chain. Fish larvae (themselves classed as zooplankton) are eating smaller zooplankton. Worms that swim by spiraling their bodies through the water are eating anything smaller than themselves.

Krill are the largest of the zooplankton. Many things eat them.

KRILL

The small shrimp species called krill are the largest of the zooplankton. These tiny animals are food for some of the largest creatures in the oceans: baleen whales. In some parts of the seas, krill have the largest biomass. That means that even though they are so small individually, the whole population together weighs more than the whole population of any other species in the area. Krill migrate to the surface with other zooplankton every night.

Some of these worms and other tiny creatures are **bioluminescent**. They use chemicals within their bodies to create light. As the sunlight fades into dusk, you can see flashes of light where the waves lap against your boat. Just as animals that live full-time in the sunless depths use light to hunt, attract mates, or protect themselves, so too do some of the animals that migrate every night.

Not every fish that lives at a great depth moves with the diel vertical migration. Some fish are so specially adapted to the coldness and intense pressure at the bottom of the ocean that they would die if they came to the surface. These often have soft, gelatinous bodies, limited muscle development, and nerves that don't react very quickly. They are made for a slower life in cold, dark water. The fish that make the nightly journey usually have strong bones and muscles, and active nervous systems. They are prepared for the fast life nearer the surface.

The female deepsea anglerfish uses a bioluminescent lure to attract prey in the dark.

Even among the species of fish that follow the zooplankton to the surface, not every member of the population rises every night. Often, a fish will rise one night and feast on the prey gathered near the surface. At dawn it will descend again, and then spend several days digesting its meal. In the cold depths, an animal's metabolism—how fast it uses its energy reserves—is much slower. One night of activity near the surface can give a fish enough food energy for several days in the deep sea.

NIGHT

IT is completely dark now. You can still see activity near the surface, of animals feeding, and you wonder, do marine animals ever sleep? You begin to investigate, starting with fish.

The question about fish sleep is a tricky one. You know that land animals are asleep when their eyes are closed and they are resting and not alert. More scientifically, land animals such as birds and mammals are asleep when a part of their brain called the neocortex has a certain pattern of electrical activity. But fish don't have a neocortex in their brains, and they don't have eyelids!

Still, most fish seem to enter a resting state that is their version of sleep. As you explore the ocean at nighttime, you will see many kinds of fish become inactive. Bottom-dwelling fish like flounder and lizardfish will often bury themselves in the sand to sleep. Fish that live in or near reefs or rocky areas will usually try to find some kind of shelter when they

Hogfish are a species that sleeps
extremely deeply.

Parrotfish make their own sleeping bags out of mucus.

sleep. Some fish are motionless for long periods of time but will still be alert if danger approaches.

Other fish seem to be almost completely unconscious when they sleep. When you find a hogfish that is deeply asleep, you discover that you can very carefully scoop your hand under its belly without it waking up. You even try gently carrying it up to the surface. The hogfish doesn't come to life until its gills are out of the water. It is one of the fish that sleeps the most deeply.

Some fish even make their own sleeping bags. If you dive down to a rocky outcrop, a reef, or even a seagrass bed at night, you might find sleeping parrotfish and wrasses nestled in a cozy bag of mucus. When they are ready to go to sleep, they begin to make mucus in their mouths. This mucus balloons out to form a bag around their entire bodies. Inside the mucus cocoon, these fish are almost invisible. Even if they are out in the open, their scent is hidden from predators, making it much less likely that sharks or other hungry fish will notice them. The mucus bubble also serves as an early warning system, a sort of fence. If a predator does notice them and starts

Nurse sharks don't have to swim all the time, and often sleep in caves or under ledges.

SACRIFICING SLEEP

Some fish that sleep under normal circumstances will suddenly stop sleeping entirely for days or weeks when they migrate or reproduce. Fish with caring parenting behavior will sometimes stop sleeping when they care for their eggs. Some eggs need constant protection, or for the parent to fan currents of water over them with their fins.

Many dolphins and whales have scars from the cookiecutter shark.

COOKIECUTTER SHARK

One strange nocturnal shark is the cookiecutter shark. This shark, which measures less than 2 feet (.6 m), feeds by swimming up to sleeping whales, dolphins, or turtles, gouging a chunk of flesh from them, and quickly fleeing. They even bite hunks out of other sharks.

investigating, they will touch the mucus first, alerting the parrotfish so it can wake up and dart to safety.

There are some exceptions. The tuna you saw earlier don't seem to ever sleep, or stop swimming at all. Neither do some other species of open-water fish such as mackerel, bluefish, and some kinds of sharks. The role of sleep isn't completely understood. Part of its purpose seems to be to let the brain file and organize memories. The things that you—or an animal—experience during the day are added to your memory so they can be remembered and used later. Some scientists think that open water fish don't need sleep to organize their daily experiences. Most of their environment is so "boring"—open water with no obstacles, objects, or even other animals most of the time—that their brain can use that boring cruising time to get organized.

You've probably heard a theory that sharks never sleep because they have to keep swimming

Baby sea turtles sleep at the surface with their flippers tucked over their shells.

to force water over their gills so they can breathe. Open ocean sharks probably recharge like tuna do, letting their brains rest during uneventful hours of swimming. While it is true that many sharks do have to swim all the time, others don't. Nurse sharks can rest on the bottom because their gills can move water while they aren't swimming. As you explore the nighttime ocean, you look for sleeping nurse sharks. But they are all wide awake! Nurse sharks, and many other kinds of sharks, are nocturnal. Other kinds of sharks can be active at any time of day, if there is prey available.

Sea turtles also sleep at night. Baby sea turtles can't hold their breath for very long, so they have to float at the surface. There they can breathe

Sea turtles return to the beach where they were born to lay their eggs.

every few minutes. They usually tuck their front flippers over the back of their shells when they sleep. Mature sea turtles, though, can hold their breath for several hours when they sleep. Some will sleep at the surface, though this puts them at greater risk from shark attack. Others, which live near shallower water, might go to a reef at night and wedge themselves in a crevice or under a rock. One loggerhead sea turtle was recorded holding its breath for seven hours.

As you start to sail back toward shore, tired from exploring the ocean, you notice that a number of loggerhead sea turtles are swimming in the same direction. You follow them back to shore. One big female nears the shore. In the water, she swam so gracefully. Now, you hear her grunt with the effort of hauling her 300-pound (136 kg) body onto the sand. She, and hundreds of other sea turtles, have returned to the same beach where they were born to lay their eggs. They have to lay their eggs at night, because the heat of the sun would exhaust them, and even kill them.

You watch the loggerhead scoop out a deep hole with her back flippers and lay more than one hundred eggs that look like ping-pong balls. In about eighty days the babies will hatch, also at night. This helps keep them safe from predators such as gulls and crabs.

The oceans of Earth are huge and deep, and your journey has shown you only a fraction of the wonders to be found every day and night in the marine world.

WHERE ARE THE OCEANS?

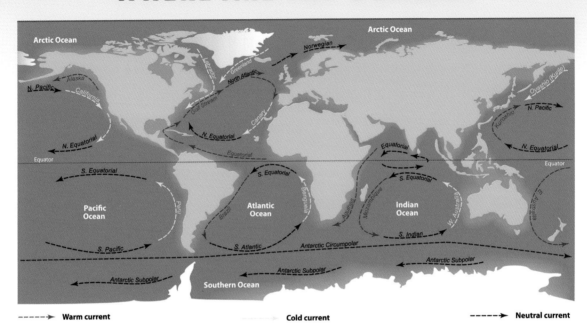

----→ **Warm current**　　　　　——→ **Cold current**　　　　　----→ **Neutral current**

FAST FACTS ABOUT OCEANS

LOCATION: There are five named oceans: the Pacific, Atlantic, Indian, Southern (or Antarctic), and Arctic. They are interconnected, and together, they form the World Ocean. In general, the word "ocean" refers to all salt water on the planet, though some might be in gulfs, bays, seas, estuaries, or other divisions smaller than the five named oceans.

SIZE: Salt water covers about 71 percent of the Earth's surface. Salt water makes up 97 percent of the planet's total water. By volume, the oceans cover about 320 million cubic miles (1.35 billion cubic kilometers). The Challenger

Deep in the area of the Pacific known as the Mariana Trench is the deepest point in the ocean, at 36,070 feet (10,994 m) below sea level.

TEMPERATURE: The world's oceans have a very wide temperature range. The average ocean surface temperature is 62.6°F (17°C). Near the equator, ocean surface temperatures can reach 80°F (27°C). Nearer the North and South Poles, surface temperature can drop to 28°F (-2°C). Salt water freezes at 28.4°F; freshwater freezes at 32°F (0°C).

RAINFALL: Since oceans cover almost three-quarters of Earth's surface, they get the majority of the planet's rainfall. Tropical parts of the ocean might receive almost 200 inches (5 m) of rain every year. About 30 percent of the rain that falls on land makes its way back to the oceans via rivers.

PLANTS FOUND IN THE OCEAN: Plants found in the sea include algae and seaweed such as kelp, sagrassum, sea lettuce, Irish moss, and red and brown algae. Closer to shore are turtle grass and eelgrass.

ANIMALS FOUND IN THE OCEAN: Some bony fish that are commonly found in the oceans include flounder, tuna, swordfish, sailfish, sardines, herring, mackerel, cod, hogfish, mullet, pufferfish, sea horses, salmon, catfish, and dolphin fish (or mahi-mahi). Some sharks found in the ocean include great whites, hammerheads, blacktip, thresher, nurse, and whale sharks. Oceangoing reptiles include sea turtles such as loggerhead, hawksbill, leatherback, and green turtles. There are also several species of venomous sea snakes. Marine mammals include dolphins such as the bottlenose dolphin and orcas, and huge whales like the blue, humpback, and sperm whales. Seals and sea lions are marine mammals that spend part of their lives on land. Dugongs live in tropical seas, and manatees travel from fresh to salt water.

GLOSSARY

agile Able to move quickly and easily.

bait ball A tight formation of small fish where each tries to stay in the middle.

baleen The tough, comb-like material some whales use to filter their food.

behemoth A huge creature.

bioluminescent Producing light inside the body by chemical means.

camouflage Using color, pattern, or shape to hide.

cold-blooded Depending on the outside environment for body temperature.

countershading A coloration in which the top is dark and the bottom is light.

crepuscular Active at dawn or twilight.

detritus Dead organic matter, including bodies or parts of bodies and fecal matter.

diurnal Active during the day.

dorsal The top side of an animal.

horizon The line where the sky and Earth seem to meet.

intertidal The part of a beach between high tide and low tide.

mammal A warm blooded animal that nurses its young.

migration Moving from one location to another, particularly long distances, usually with seasonal change.

nematocyst The stinging cell of a jellyfish tentacle.

nocturnal Active during the night.

nutrients Something that gives nourishment so an organism can grow.

ocean A large expanse of salt water.

pelagic Living in the open ocean.

phytoplankton Plant-like plankton.

plankton The small plants and animals that drift with currents.

pod A group of dolphins or whales.

predator An animal that hunts other animals for food.

prey An animal that is hunted by other animals for food.

schools Large groups of one species of fish.

sonar Something that measures shape and distance using reflected sound waves.

tentacle The arm-like structure of a jellyfish, squid, or octopus.

territory The area that an animal has established as its own.

toxic Something that contains a substance that can cause harm or death.

twilight The time between daylight and darkness, either just before sunset or just before sunrise.

warm-blooded An animal whose temperature is controlled internally.

zooplankton Animal plankton such as small shrimp.

FIND OUT MORE

Books

Dinwiddie, Robert. *Oceans: The Definitive Guide*. New York: DK, 2014.

Discovery Channel. *Discovery Channel Sharkopedia*. New York: Discovery/Time, 2013.

Marsh, Laura. *Sea Turtles*. Washington, DC: National Geographic Children's Books, 2011.

Papastavrou, Vassili. *Whale*. New York: DK Children, 2004.

Websites

California State University: Ocean Life for Kids

http://web.calstatela.edu/faculty/eviau/edit557/oceans/linda/loceans.htm

The California State University has information about all kinds of ocean creatures. It also has activities like quizzes and a make-a-fish project.

National Geographic Kids: Ocean Facts

http://www.ngkids.co.uk/science-and-nature/Ocean-Facts

This site run by National Geographic has some crazy and interesting facts about the world's oceans, links to related content, and a video feature that shows animals that are masters of disguise.

Science Kids: Shark Facts for Kids

http://www.sciencekids.co.nz/sciencefacts/animals/shark.html

This popular science site from New Zealand has lots of fun shark facts. It also has links to many other science subjects.

INDEX

Page numbers in boldface are illustrations.
Entries in boldface are glossary terms.

ABOUT THE AUTHOR

Laura L. Sullivan is the author of more than forty fiction and nonfiction books for children, including the fantasies *Under the Green Hill* and *Guardian of the Green Hill.* She has written many books for Cavendish Square, including two titles in the A Day in an Ecosystem series.

PHOTO CREDITS